TEN APPLES UP ON TOP

By

Dr. Seuss

writing as

Theo. LeSieg

Illustrated by Roy McKie

HarperCollins *Children's Books*

™ & © Dr. Seuss Enterprises, L.P.
All Rights Reserved

A CIP catalogue record for this title is available from the
British Library.
No part of this publication may be reproduced, stored
in a retrieval system or transmitted in any form or by
any means, electronic, mechanical, photocopying,
recording or otherwise, without the prior permission of
HarperCollins Publishers Ltd, 1 London Bridge Street
London SE1 9GF

1 3 5 7 9 10 8 6 4 2

ISBN 978-0-00-823999-2

© 1961 by Random House, Inc.
™ & © renewed 1989 by Dr. Seuss Enterprises, L.P.
and Roy McKie
All Rights Reserved
Published by arrangement with Random House Inc.,
New York, USA
First published in the UK 1963
This edition published in the UK 2017 by
HarperCollins *Children's Books,*
a division of HarperCollins*Publishers* Ltd
1 London Bridge Street
London SE1 9GF

www.harpercollins.co.uk

Printed in China

PART OF A SET. NOT FOR INDIVIDUAL RESALE

One apple
up on top!

Two apples
up on top!

Look, you.

I can do it, too.

Look!

See!

I can do three!

Three . . .

Three . . .

I see.

I see.

You can do three
but I can do more.
You have three
but I have four.

Look! See, now.

I can hop

with four apples

up on top.

And I can hop

up on a tree

with four apples

up on me.

Look here, you two.

See here, you two.

I can get five

on top.

Can you?

I am so good
I will not stop.
Five!
Now six!
Now seven on top!

Seven apples
up on top!

20

I am

so good

they will not drop.

Five, six, seven!
Fun, fun, fun!
Seven, six, five,
four, three, two, one!

But, see!
We are as good as you.
Look! Now we
have seven, too.

And now, see here.

Eight! Eight on top!

Eight apples up!

Not one will drop.

27

Eight! Eight!
And we can skate.
Look now!
We can skate
with eight.

But I can do nine.
And hop!
And drink!
You can not do this,
I think.

We can! We can!

We can do it, too.

See here.

We are as good as you!

We all are very good
I think.
With nine, we all
can hop and drink.

34

Nine is very good.

But then . . .

Come on and we

will make it ten!

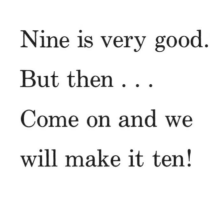

Look!

Ten

apples

up

on

top!

We are not

going to let them drop!

Look out!

Look out!

I see a mop.

I will make
the apples fall.
Get out. Get out. You!
One and all!

Come on! Come on!
Come down this hall.
We must not let
our apples fall!

43

Out of our way!
We can not stop.
We can not let
our apples drop.

This is not good.
What will we do?
They want to get
our apples, too.

48

They will get them
if we let them.
Come! We can not
let them get them.

50

Look out!

The mop!

The mop!

The mop!

You can not stop
our apple fun.
Our apples will not drop.
Not one!

Come on! Come on!
Come one! Come all!
We have to make
the apples fall.

They must not get
our apples down.
Come on! Come on!
Get out of town!

Apples!

Apples up on top!

All of this

must stop

STOP

STOP!

Now all our fun
is going to stop!
Our apples all
are going to drop.

Look!
Ten apples
on us all!

What fun!
We will not
let them fall.